# Thoughtful Alphabets
## THE JUST DESSERT & THE DEADLY BLOTTER

EDWARD GOREY

Pomegranate
PORTLAND, OREGON

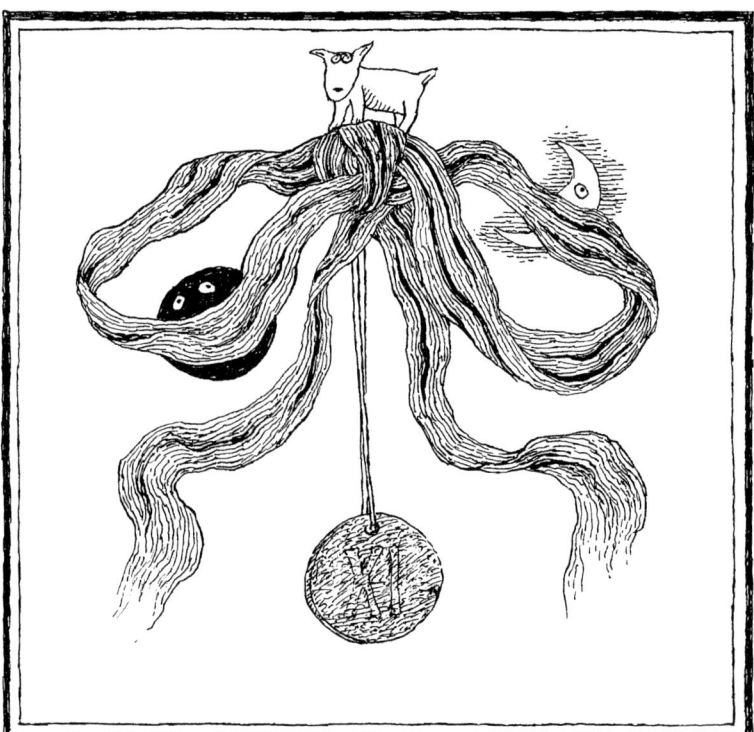

# THE JUST DESSERT
*Thoughtful Alphabet XI*

## EDWARD GOREY

Nevertheless.

One piddling question remains.

Vilify.

Yes.

# THE DEADLY BLOTTER

*Edward Gorey*

THOUGHTFUL ALPHABET XVII

*Alarming behaviour.*

*Corpse.*

*Detective enters.*

*Fearful glances.*

*Helpful irrelevancies.*

Jitters.

*Knitting.*

*Likely motives.*

*Notable omissions.*

*Pointed questions.*

*Reluctance.*

*Subtle trap.*

*Unmasked villain.*

*Extenuation yields zero.*

Published by Pomegranate Communications, Inc.
19018 NE Portal Way, Portland OR 97230
800 227 1428 • www.pomegranate.com

Pomegranate Europe Ltd.
Unit 1, Heathcote Business Centre, Hurlbutt Road
Warwick, Warwickshire CV34 6TD, UK
[+44] 0 1926 430111 • sales@pomeurope.co.uk

An **Edward Gorey**® licensed product. © 1997 Edward Gorey.
Published under license from The Edward Gorey Charitable Trust.
All rights reserved.

The contents of this book are protected by copyright, including all images and all text. This copyrighted material may not be reproduced or transmitted in any form or by any means, electronic or mechanical, including but not limited to photocopying, scanning, recording, or by any information storage or retrieval system, without the express permission in writing of the copyright holders.

This edition first published by Pomegranate Communications, Inc., 2012.

Library of Congress Control Number: 2012935394
ISBN 978-0-7649-6336-0

Pomegranate Catalog No. A213

Designed by Gina Bostian

To learn about new releases and special offers from Pomegranate,
please sign up for our e-mail newsletter at www.pomegranate.com.
For all other queries, see "Contact Us" on our home page.

Printed in Korea

22 21 20 19 18 17 16 15 14 13   11 10 9 8 7 6 5 4 3 2

OTHER EDWARD GOREY BOOKS PUBLISHED BY POMEGRANATE:

*The Awdrey-Gore Legacy*
*The Black Doll: A Silent Screenplay*
*The Blue Aspic*
*Category: Fifty Drawings*
*The Donald Boxed Set: Donald and the . . . and Donald Has a Difficulty*, text by Peter F. Neumeyer
*The Dong with a Luminous Nose*, text by Edward Lear
*The Eclectic Abecedarium*
*Edward Gorey: The New Poster Book*
*Elegant Enigmas: The Art of Edward Gorey*, by Karen Wilkin
*Elephant House: Or, the Home of Edward Gorey*, by Kevin McDermott
*The Evil Garden*
*Floating Worlds: The Letters of Edward Gorey and Peter F. Neumeyer*
*The Gilded Bat*
*The Hapless Child*
*The Jumblies*, text by Edward Lear
*The Lost Lions*
*The Osbick Bird*
*The Remembered Visit: A Story Taken from Life*
*The Sopping Thursday*
*Three Classic Children's Stories: Little Red Riding Hood, Jack the Giant-Killer, and Rumpelstiltskin*, text by James Donnelly
*The Treehorn Trilogy: The Shrinking of Treehorn, Treehorn's Treasure, and Treehorn's Wish*, text by Florence Parry Heide
*The Twelve Terrors of Christmas*, text by John Updike
*The Utter Zoo: An Alphabet* by Edward Gorey
*Why We Have Day and Night*, text by Peter F. Neumeyer
*The Wuggly Ump*

AND DON'T MISS:
*Edward Gorey's Dracula: A Toy Theatre*
*The Fantod Pack*
*The Wuggly Ump and Other Delights Coloring Book*

## ABOUT THE AUTHOR

Edward Gorey (1925–2000) is famous for the bounty of books he wrote and illustrated. His distinctive humor and astonishingly detailed crosshatch ink drawings brought to life more than one hundred works. Gorey also was a playwright, an award-winning set and costume designer, and the creator of the animated introduction to the PBS series *Mystery!*